For Melanie, Eva and Claudia

Published 1997 exclusively for
Early Learning Centre
South Marston Park
Swindon SN3 4TJ
by Walker Books Ltd
87 Vauxhall Walk
London SE11 5HJ

2 4 6 8 10 9 7 5 3

© 1997 Clara Vulliamy

Printed in Hong Kong

ISBN 0-7445-2909-3

Friends

Clara Vulliamy

Early Learning Centre   WALKER BOOKS

Nida lived next door to Jake.
There was a gap in the fence between their gardens, just big enough for Nida to squeeze through when she came to play.

"Let's go exploring at the end of your garden,"
said Nida. "It's a great big scary jungle down
there! We can look for creepy-crawlies and put
them in a jar. And maybe there's a tiger hiding
in the bushes."
"We can make a tent and stay there for ever,"
said Jake, although he wasn't too sure he
wanted to meet a tiger.

They packed Jake's rucksack with all the
things they would need.
They found a sheet to use as a tent, and
some blankets and cushions to go inside it.

Nida fetched a fishing-net
from the toy box, in case
they needed to catch some
wild animals.
"I'll carry the fishing-net,"
said Jake.
"I had it first," said Nida.

Jake found the toy buggy for his rabbit
to ride in, and they set off for the
bottom of the garden.

Then Nida said, "It's Mouse's turn
to ride in the buggy. Give it to me."
She grabbed it and pulled.
"No, it's mine!" said
Jake, hanging on.

The buggy toppled over ...

and so did Nida and Jake.

Jake ran off and hid in the bushes. He was cross and didn't want to share his things.

He watched Nida trying to make the tent
on her own.

Then he heard a rustling noise in the leaves.
It must be the tiger! Jake was very scared.
He ran to Nida as fast as he could.

"I can hear the tiger – it's there, in the bushes!"
Nida was scared too.

As they stared at the place where the noise was coming from, out stepped Jake's old ginger cat.

He came lazily over and rubbed
against their legs, wanting to be stroked.

At last they managed to make their tent.
It was cosy and snug inside.

"I'm cooking sausages for our tea over the campfire," said Jake.

"And I'm keeping the wild animals away," said Nida. "This time we're looking out for CROCODILES!"